Pixie Tricks

The Halloween Goblin

Catch all of the Pixie Tricks adventures!

Sprite's Secret

• • •

The Greedy Gremlin

• • •

The Pet Store Sprite

• • •

The Halloween Goblin

PIXIE TRICKS

The Halloween Goblin

· by ·

TRACEY WEST

A LITTLE APPLE PAPERBACK

SCHOLASTIC INC.
New York Toronto London Auckland Sydney
Mexico City New Delhi Hong Kong

For Katie. Thanks for all your help,

encouragement, and inspiration.

— T.W.

Book design by Dawn Adelman

ISBN 0-439-17980-7

Cover illustration by James Bernardin.
Interior and sticker illustrations by Thea Kliros.

12 11 5/0

Printed in the U.S.A. 40
First Scholastic printing, September 2000

Contents

Sprite is a Pixie Tricker,

Sent by the fairy queen.

He's after fourteen pixies.

They're troublesome and mean!

Sprite asked for help from Violet,

A clever little girl.

She'll help him trick the pixies,

And return them to their world.

So far they've tricked three pixies,

With eleven more to go.

Will Sprite and Violet trick some more?

Keep reading and you'll know!

Chapter One
Monster Magic

"What do you mean, a wizard is after us?"

Violet Briggs sighed. She and her cousin Leon were walking to school. She had told the story to Leon over and over. He just didn't get it.

Violet's friend Sprite, a tiny fairy, flew in front of Leon's face. "Finn is a fairy wizard," Sprite explained. "He is one of the fourteen troublemaking pixies who escaped from my world. He led the escape."

"I get that part," Leon said, wrinkling his freckled nose. "But why is he after us?"

"Because he found out that Sprite has come here to send the pixies back to their world," Violet answered.

Sprite nodded. "Finn's angry. We already tricked three pixies and sent them back to the Otherworld. He will try to stop us so we don't trick any more. Finn wants the pixies to stay here and cause more trouble."

Sometimes Violet couldn't believe they had already tricked three pixies. First Pix. Then Jolt. Then Aquamarina.

"Right," Violet said. "Finn liked it when Pix made people play instead of work. And Jolt made video games get messed up. And Aquamarina made faucets leak and turned people into fish. He didn't like it when we stopped them."

"Maybe we should just tell that wizard that we'll stop tricking pixies," Leon said. "Then he'll leave us alone."

"You know we can't do that," Violet told Leon. "There are eleven more pixies to trick. Like Hinky Pink, the one who changes the weather. We've got to trick him and all the others."

"Besides," Sprite added. "I can't go back home to the Otherworld until my job is done. I could never face the fairy queen. She's counting on me."

Violet smiled at Sprite. She knew he would never give up.

Violet reached out and let Sprite sit on her finger. "You'd better get in my back-pack," she said. "We're almost at school."

Violet looked up ahead. A crowd of

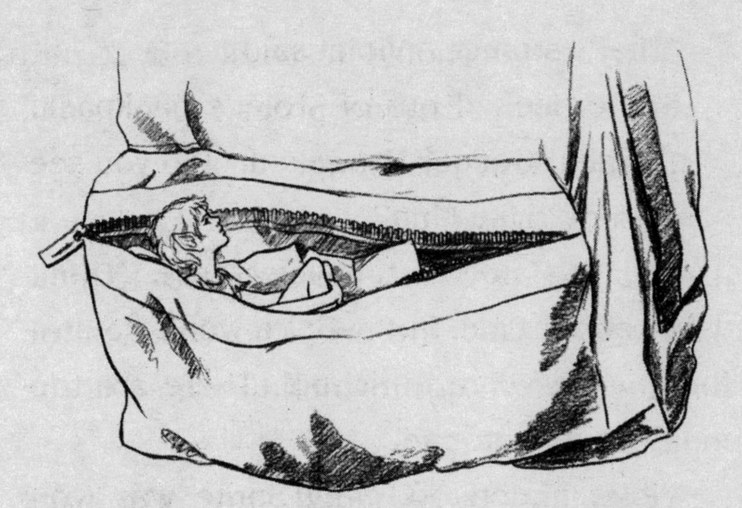

children waited behind the crossing guard, Mrs. Stacy. She held them all back.

"Wait here," Mrs. Stacy said nervously. "Crossing the street is very dangerous. Cars racing. Trucks zooming. Watch out! Watch out!"

But there wasn't a single car or truck in sight.

"That's strange," Violet said.

Sprite peeked out of Violet's backpack.

"What's strange?" he asked. "Did you see something? Like Finn?"

"No, it's not that," Violet said. "Don't worry about Finn. I'm sure he won't do anything while we're in school. There are too many people around."

Violet understood why Sprite was worried. Finn was a powerful wizard. But Violet wasn't concerned about Finn right now. She was in a good mood today. Her mom had bought her a brand-new shirt to wear. Violet liked it because it had a pretty purple flower.

"It's the same color as your eyes," her mom had said.

Violet looked down at her shirt.

And she screamed!

Chapter Two
Monster Alert!

Instead of a pretty purple flower, there was a purple monster face on Violet's shirt! The face had long fangs. It had bulging eyes. Slime dripped from its hairy ears.

Sprite stuck his head out of the backpack. "What's the matter?" he asked.

"My shirt," Violet cried. "Look!"

"Blaaaaah!" The monster face moved! It stuck out its tongue.

"Yikes!" yelled Violet.

"Cool," Leon said. "Nice monster."

"It is not cool," Violet told Leon. She grabbed her cousin by the arm and pulled him to the edge of the sidewalk. She didn't want anyone else to see her shirt.

"Leon," Violet said, "my shirt is *moving*! Something's going on here!"

Sprite flew out of the backpack. "I knew it!" he said.

There was a rustling sound. They looked around. Something moved in a bush next to them.

"Happy Halloween!" a voice growled.

There was a flash of gray, and a small creature darted out of the bush. It ran out of sight.

"Bogey Bill!" Sprite cried. "I should have known."

"Bogey who?" Leon asked. "And why did he say, 'Happy Halloween'? It's not Halloween yet."

"Bill is a goblin. He likes things that are scary," Sprite said. "He wishes every day were Halloween. And he likes to make people scared of normal things. Like when you're afraid to look under your bed."

Violet looked down at the monster face. "Well, the scary part explains my shirt. Can we fix it?"

Sprite fluttered his wings. "I'm not sure," he said.

"What if I said Bogey Bill's name backwards three times?" Violet asked. "That has stopped pixie magic before."

"You could try," Sprite said.

Violet took a deep breath.

"Llib Yegob!

"Llib Yegob!

"Llib — hic!"

"Hic?" Sprite asked. "Violet, you said it wrong."

Violet moaned. "I — hic — know!" she said. "I have the hiccups!"

Chapter Three
Hic — Trouble!

Violet looked down at her shirt. It hadn't changed back.

The monster face laughed at her.

"What — hic — should I do now?" she cried.

Leon swung his backpack over his shoulder. "That's your problem," he said. "I don't want to be late."

Leon ran off.

The purple monster face burped loudly.

"I can't go to school like this," Violet moaned.

"It's not so bad," Sprite said, trying to smile. "We'll get Bogey Bill after school. I promise."

Violet nodded. "Hic. Okay." She crossed her arms in front of her shirt.

When Violet got to class, she tapped her friend Brittany on the shoulder.

"Eeeeeek!" Brittany shrieked. She spun around.

"Oh, Violet," she said, "it's you. You scared me."

"Sorry, Brittany," Violet said.

Brittany sure is jumpy, Violet thought. *So was the crossing guard. Could it be Bogey Bill at work?*

Violet slid into her seat. Then she opened her desktop and slipped Sprite inside. She made sure no one saw him.

Violet used an eraser to hold open the desktop a tiny crack.

"Hic. Are you all right?" Violet whispered into the desk.

Sprite sat down on the side of Violet's pencil box.

"There's not much to do here," Sprite whispered back. "But that's okay. I've got to think about how to trick Bogey Bill."

Sprite took a tiny book from his bag. The *Book of Tricks.* The book told how to trick the escaped pixies.

"Good luck. Hic!" Violet said.

The bell rang, and Violet's teacher, Ms. Rose, led them in the Pledge of Allegiance. Violet liked Ms. Rose. She always wore bright colors. And she smiled a lot.

But today Ms. Rose wasn't smiling. She looked nervous. She tapped her fingers on the desk.

"David, can you please go the supply closet for me?" Ms. Rose asked a student.

The dark-haired boy looked scared. He stared at the closet door. He didn't move.

"Ms. Rose, do I have to?" David asked.

SPIDER
BAT
PUMPKIN

"Is something wrong?" the teacher asked.

"Uh, no," David said. He looked pale. "I — I just don't want to."

Ms. Rose smiled nervously. "Who would like to open the closet door for me?"

No one in the class answered. They all looked scared.

Ms. Rose took a deep breath. "I guess I'll do it myself, then," she said.

Ms. Rose walked to the closet. She grabbed the doorknob.

Violet turned her head. She couldn't look. She was scared, but she didn't know why.

None of the kids in class could look, either.

Ms. Rose slowly turned the knob. She opened the door.

Then she smiled with relief. "See, class?" she said. "Nothing to be scared of."

Violet turned around. There was nothing in the closet but paper and paint.

Ms. Rose picked up some orange and black paper.

"Today we will make Halloween decorations," the teacher told the class. She started to pass out the paper.

Halloween decorations? Halloween wasn't for weeks and weeks, Violet thought.

"It is never too early to celebrate Halloween," Ms. Rose said, as if she'd read Violet's mind.

Violet gasped. Bogey Bill must have been here!

The teacher looked at Violet. "I see Violet is in the Halloween spirit. What a lovely shirt, Violet."

The monster face wiggled its ears at Ms. Rose. The teacher jumped back.

"I think I need to sit down," Ms. Rose said.

The class turned around and looked at Violet's monster shirt. Luckily, the face kept still.

"Hic! It's nothing special. Hic!" Violet said.

Some of the kids giggled.

Violet wanted to sink into her seat. She couldn't get rid of the weird monster shirt. And she couldn't get rid of her hiccups, either.

"Violet has the hiccups!" Evan Peters chanted.

Ms. Rose frowned. "It's not nice to tease, Evan. Please apologize to Violet."

Evan rolled his eyes. "Sorry, Violet. Hic!"

Ms. Rose looked angry. "Evan, I warned you!"

But Evan looked shocked. "Hic! I really do have the hiccups. Hic!"

Suddenly, the room was filled with the sound of hiccups.

"Hic!"

"Hic!"

"Hic!"

Violet couldn't believe it. A whole class with the hiccups? It sounded like fairy magic to her.

Violet had to talk to Sprite. She carefully lifted up her desktop.

The class was too busy hiccuping to notice.

"Sprite!" Violet whispered. "What — hic — is going on? Is it Bogey Bill?"

Sprite looked worried.

"Bogey Bill is making everyone afraid," Sprite said. "But he doesn't cause hiccups."

"Hic! So who does?" Violet asked.

"I'm not sure," Sprite said. "But it looks like we might have to trick two pixies this time!"

Chapter Four
Lunchtime Surprise

Violet's class hiccuped and made Halloween decorations all morning. Finally, it was time for lunch.

Violet slipped Sprite into her lunch bag. She wanted to go somewhere and talk to him. But her friends Brittany and Tina ran up to her as they walked to the lunchroom.

Violet's two friends were different in some ways. Brittany had blond hair and a loud voice. Tina had dark curly hair. She was quiet and a little shy.

But both of them were Violet's good friends.

"Hic! Can you believe Ms. Rose?" Brittany asked. "She made us make Halloween decorations. Hic!"

"They were so — hic — scary!" Tina said. "I'm afraid to go back to class."

"Tina, I thought you loved Halloween. Hic!" Violet said.

"Hic! I know," Tina said. "But I can't help it! I can't look at those decorations."

Violet wished she could tell her friends what she knew. But she had to keep Sprite's secret. "Well, it was a little weird. Hic!" was all she said.

The three friends sat down at their usual

Hinky Pink–Cloud

Sport

Hinky Pink

Aquamarina on Dry Ground

Bogey Bill–T-Shirt

Buttercup–Hiccup

ISBN 0-439-22197-8 Illustration by Thea Kliros.

table. Violet looked around. The sound of hiccups filled the lunchroom.

Kids were trying all kinds of things to get rid of their hiccups. They were holding their noses and drinking milk. One boy was standing on his head.

Then, suddenly, the hiccups stopped.

And everyone started screaming!

Violet looked around the lunchroom. All the kids were scared and afraid.

"My Jell-O's alive!" shouted one girl. "It's coming to get me!"

"There's a monster under my table!" someone screamed.

"There are worms in my spaghetti!" yelled another kid.

One boy buried his head in his books. "I can't go back to class," he said. "I'm afraid the teacher's going to call on me!"

But there were no worms. Or monsters. Everyone was letting their fears get the better of them.

"Eeeeeek!"

The screams grew louder.

Brittany and Tina hugged each other.

"I'm afraid of all this screaming!" Brittany said.

Violet had to talk to Sprite. She grabbed her lunch bag. Then she ran out the lunchroom door.

"Sprite!" she said. "Hic! Is Bogey Bill behind this?"

Sprite flew up to the top of the bag.

"Of course," Sprite said. He opened the *Book of Tricks*. "Here's what I've found so far."

Violet saw two pages about Bogey Bill. There was a blank space where his picture should be. Violet knew that the picture would reappear when Bogey Bill was tricked.

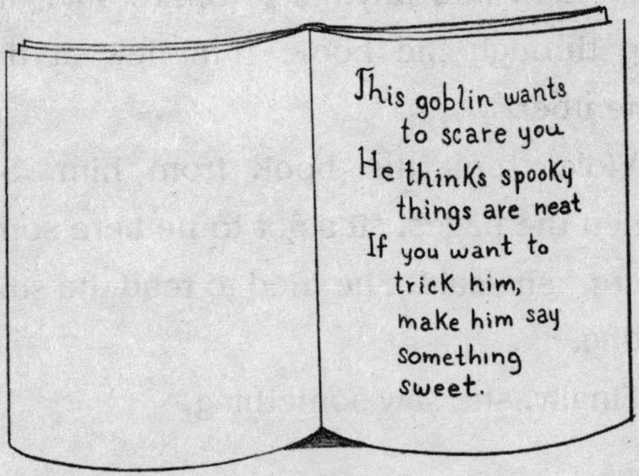

There was also a rhyme. Violet read it aloud.

"'This goblin wants to scare you.
He thinks spooky things are neat.
If you want to trick him,
Make him say something sweet.' Hic!"

Violet sighed. "Hic! What about the hiccups?"

"I can't find anything," Sprite said, flipping through the book. "I'm new at this, remember?"

Violet took the book from him. She turned the pages. "It's got to be here somewhere," she said. She tried to read the small writing.

Finally, she saw something.

"How about this one?" Violet asked. "She's a sprite named Buttercup. Her rhyme says,

"'She will give you the hiccups,
Anytime or anywhere.
To trick this shifty sprite,
You must give her a big scare!'

"That makes sense," Violet said. "A good scare is one way to get rid of hiccups."

Sprite frowned. "There's just one problem. We've seen Buttercup's *magic*, but we haven't exactly seen *her*. We'll have to find her before we can *trick* her."

Violet sighed. This was not going to be easy!

Chapter Five
Snakes Alive!

It took almost an hour for the teachers to calm things down in the lunchroom. Soon everyone was back in class.

Only Violet knew what had really happened. What horrible thing would Bogey Bill do next?

The one good thing Violet noticed was that most kids had had their hiccups scared away by their fears. Except for Violet. She was still hiccuping when the dismissal bell rang.

Leon ran up to her outside.

"Did you see what happened in the lunchroom?" he asked. "That was Bogey Bill, right?"

Sprite peeked out of the backpack.

"We think so," Violet said.

"Then we've got to get him right now!"

Leon said. "He could make the whole town go crazy with fear."

"Yes, Violet," Sprite said. "We must hurry."

"I can't," Violet said. "Hic! I promised Tina I'd help watch her baby sister."

Sprite looked nervous. "But there's no time for that," he said. "I'm a Royal Pixie Tricker. I've got to do my job."

"I know," Violet said. "But I'm just a little girl. Hic! I can't look for fairies all the time. Besides, I promised."

Sprite sighed. "I suppose."

Leon shrugged. "Do what you want. I'm going to go hide in my room!" He ran off.

"Violet!" Brittany called out. She and Tina were waiting on the corner. "Come and walk with us!"

Violet tucked Sprite into her backpack.

"Hic! We'll look tomorrow, I promise," she said.

When they got to Tina's house, Tina's mother handed Tina her baby sister. Linda had dark curly hair like Tina. She had big brown eyes.

"Thanks for watching Linda, sweetie," Ms. Ramos said. "I have some work to do upstairs."

Violet and Brittany followed Tina into the playroom. Tina put Linda into a playpen and plopped down on the floor.

Linda grabbed a stuffed pink bunny and hugged it.

Violet knelt down. "Hic! What a cute bunny, Linda," Violet said. "Hic!"

The baby laughed at the sound of Violet's hiccups.

"That reminds me," Tina said. "Linda's favorite show is on."

Tina picked up a remote control and turned on the TV. A person in a big pink bunny outfit was singing a nursery rhyme.

"What's this?" Violet asked.

Brittany rolled her eyes. "It's *The Fluffy Bunny Baby Show,*" she said. "My little brother watches it all the time. It drives me crazy."

"Linda loves it," Tina said. "So do all the kids in her play group. Tomorrow is the big *Fluffy Bunny Baby* special. They're all going to watch it together."

"I know," said Brittany. "My aunt works at the TV station. They're doing it live."

The Fluffy Bunny sang the song again.

Baby Linda smiled and clapped.

Brittany held her ears. "I can't stand it!"

But Violet smiled. She'd rather watch a fluffy pink bunny than look for a scary fairy. This was a lot safer.

"Hic! I like Fluffy Bunny," Violet said. "Don't you, Linda?" Violet turned to her.

Then she gasped.

The toy bunny in Linda's hands had changed.

Now it was a stuffed snake!

Linda saw Violet's shocked face. She looked at her stuffed toy.

Then she began to wail. "Waaaaaaaaah!"

Tina picked her up. "What's this?" she asked, picking up the snake. She looked angry. "I bet Ricky did this! That brother of mine is always playing jokes."

"Well, it's not very funny," Brittany sniffed.

But Violet knew the truth.

Bogey Bill had struck again!

Chapter Six
Queen Mab

The next morning, Violet and Sprite met under the oak tree in her backyard.

"No school today," Violet said. "Now we can look for Bogey Bill. Hic! I don't want him to scare anybody else."

Sprite flew onto Violet's shoulder. "We should find Buttercup, too. You need to get rid of those hiccups."

"I know," Violet said. "But Bill is worse. Hic!"

Just then, Violet noticed something. A purple glow came from Sprite's magic bag.

"The fairy queen!" Violet said. "She can help us. Hic!" Queen Mab had helped them the last time they had a problem.

Sprite opened the bag and took out a small stone. The stone glowed brightly.

The light on the stone faded. Then a picture began to appear.

It was Queen Mab. Violet had forgotten how beautiful she was. She had long red hair and purple eyes.

Sprite and Violet bowed.

"What is wrong, Sprite and Violet?" asked the fairy queen.

Sprite lowered his eyes. "We're a little, um, confused," he said. "There are two pixies causing trouble at the same time."

"We don't know what to do," Violet added. "Hic!"

"We've got to trick Bogey Bill and Buttercup!" said Sprite. "And Bogey Bill is so scary."

Queen Mab thought. "Bogey Bill is very creepy," she said. "But I know someone who is not afraid of Bill. Robert B. Gnome can help you."

"Who is he?" Sprite asked. "And how do we find him?"

The queen's picture faded. In its place was a picture of a tiny little man. He looked nice and chubby. He had a smiling face and bright blue eyes. A white beard covered his chin. And he wore a pointy red cap on his head. He was in a garden of pretty flowers.

They could still hear the queen's voice. "Robert is a good fairy. He has lived in your world for years," she said. "Go to him. He can help you."

Then the picture on the stone faded.

"I still don't know what to do!" Sprite wailed.

"I do!" Violet said. "I've seen that gnome before. Hic!"

"Then what are we waiting for?" Sprite asked. "Let's find Robert B. Gnome!"

Chapter Seven
Robert B. Gnome

"Mrs. Wilson has the nicest garden in town," Violet explained. "It's just around the corner."

Sprite followed Violet out of her backyard. Soon they came to a tiny white house. The house was surrounded by many colorful flowers.

A small statue stood in front of a rosebush. The statue looked just like the gnome

Queen Mab had shown them. He had a red cap. A big smile. A white beard.

"There's only one problem," Sprite said. "He's not real!"

The gnome stood still. His arms were raised in the air.

Violet knelt down next to the statue. "Hic! It has to be him. It looks just like him."

Sprite flew in front of the statue's face. "I know a gnome when I see one. And this is not a —"

"Achoo!"

Violet jumped back. "Did that statue just sneeze?" she asked.

"Achoo!"

It was definitely the statue. The little man moved his arms. He scratched his nose.

"Those wings of yours sure are ticklish," he said in a jolly voice.

"Robert B. Gnome!" Violet said. "I knew it was you!"

The gnome grinned. "Sorry I didn't introduce myself sooner. I'm usually careful to stay still in front of humans. But then I saw you talking to this little fellow here."

"I'm Sprite," Sprite said. "I'm a Royal Pixie Tricker."

Robert B. Gnome frowned. "You're not here for me, are you? I'm allowed to live out here. Queen Mab said so."

"No," Violet said quickly. "Don't worry. Hic! We're not here to get you. Hic! We need your help."

She and Sprite told the gnome about Bogey Bill and Buttercup.

Robert B. Gnome stroked his beard. "That Bogey Bill," he said, shaking his head. "He and I grew up together. I knew that goblin when he couldn't even scare a grasshopper."

"We know what we're supposed to do to trick them," Sprite said. "But we're not exactly sure how to do it."

"Hic! And we don't know where to find them, either," Violet said. "We saw Bogey Bill for a — hic — second. And we've — hic — never seen Buttercup."

Robert B. Gnome stroked his beard some more.

"You've got two pixies to trick," he said. "That's double trouble."

"You can say that again," Sprite said.

"But it's also double good," Robert B. Gnome said. "You can use their powers against each other."

"Hic!" Violet said. "How do we do that?"

"Oh, you'll know," said the gnome.

"You'll know. You look like a bright little girl to me."

Robert B. Gnome took off his red cap. He rummaged through it. Then he pulled something out. "Take this," he said. He handed Violet a small stuffed toy. A spider. "You might be able to use it."

"Hic! Thanks," Violet said. "I think. But where should we go now?"

"If I were Bogey Bill, I'd probably be in the scariest place in town," the gnome replied.

Sprite's wings fluttered faster than ever. "Can't you tell us more? I'm so confused."

But Robert B. Gnome just smiled. "You'll be just fine," he said. "Now I've got to get back to guarding Mrs. Wilson's garden."

And suddenly the gnome was as still as a statue again.

"This is terrible," Sprite said. "What are we supposed to do with a stuffed spider? And how are we supposed to bring the two fairies together?"

Violet frowned. "Sprite, you should know what to do. That's your job, isn't it?"

Sprite looked at his pointy shoes. "I know," he said. "I know. But I'm trying my best."

"Of course you are," Violet said. Then, suddenly, her face lit up. "I know where to start! Robert B. Gnome said to look in the scariest place in town. Hic! There's an old house near the park. It's the spookiest place around."

"Great," Sprite mumbled. "We'll go to the spooky house, and then Bogey Bill will scare — *aaaaah!*"

Something jumped out in front of them!

Chapter Eight
The Haunted House

"So you tried to sneak off without me!"

Violet relaxed. It wasn't Bogey Bill.

It was Leon.

"You were asleep," Violet said. "I can't help it if you're lazy."

"Well, at least I'm smart," Leon said. "Smart enough to follow you."

"Well, we're smart, too," Violet said. She explained how Queen Mab had told them to go see Robert B. Gnome. Violet told Leon what Robert B. Gnome had said.

She showed Leon the stuffed spider. "I'm still not sure what to do with this toy," she said.

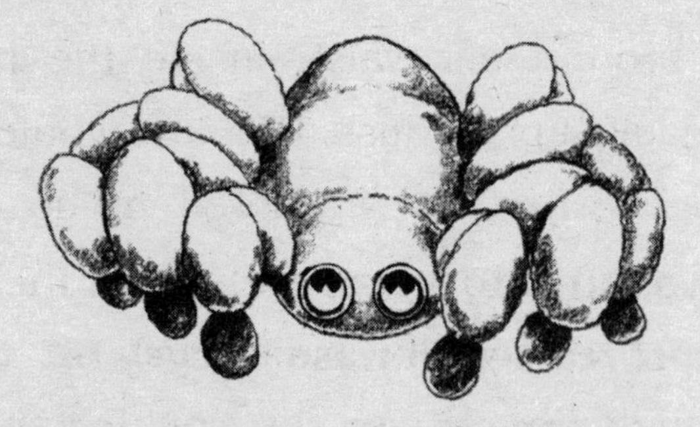

"I'll take it," Leon said. "It's cool."

Violet handed him the spider. "Let's go to that haunted house by the park. I think I know what to do."

Then Violet stopped. "Hey! My hiccups are gone!"

"That's right!" Sprite said.

"It's because I scared you," Leon said. "You should thank me."

"I will thank you," she said. "Now I know how to trick Buttercup. Let's go to the haunted house!"

Sprite reached for the little pouch that hung around his waist. Inside the pouch was magical pixie dust. The dust would take them anywhere they wanted to go. In a flash.

Sprite threw the pixie dust on them. Violet held her nose so she wouldn't sneeze.

Violet's body tingled. Then the backyard disappeared.

Now they were standing in front of Joe's Pet Store. White mice played in a cage in the front window.

"Sprite, I said *house,*" Violet said. "Not *mouse.*"

Sprite blushed a deep shade of green. "Right," he said. "Sorry about that."

Sprite threw the pixie dust again.

This time, they appeared in front of a tall house. It looked old and gray. Long stairs led up to the front door.

Violet and Leon walked up the creaky steps. Sprite flew alongside.

They opened the door and walked into a dark room. The room was filled with dusty furniture. An old piano sat against one wall. A chandelier hung from the ceiling.

"This is the perfect place for Bogey Bill," Violet whispered.

Suddenly, a cold wind blew through the room. The window shades flapped up and down. The piano played a tune all by itself. The chandelier swung back and forth.

Sprite hid behind one of Violet's braids. "You were right, Violet," he said. "Bogey Bill is here!"

Chapter Nine
Bye-bye, Buttercup

"Great," Violet whispered to Sprite and Leon. "Now we just need to get Buttercup here."

"How are you going to do that?" Leon asked.

Violet looked at her cousin. "I have a plan," she whispered.

"Hey, my hiccups are gone!" Violet said in her loudest voice. "Boy, I'm so happy I don't have hiccups!"

Nothing happened.

Violet raised her voice.

"No more hiccups for me!" she said. "I'm so lucky!"

Suddenly, there was a flash of light. A tiny sprite appeared in the air in front of them.

Violet was amazed each time she saw a fairy. This one was very pretty. She had dark hair and skin the color of a nutshell. She wore a dress made of yellow flower petals. She had dainty green slippers.

"Buttercup!" Violet cried.

"Stop that right now!" said the fairy, fluttering her shiny wings. "Hiccups are wonderful. They're beautiful. I love hiccups!"

"I hate them," Violet said. "I'm glad to be rid of them."

Buttercup frowned. She stomped her tiny foot in the air.

"What a terrible thing to say," she said.

"I'll give you the hiccups again. I'll show you how nice they are!"

A silver wand popped into Buttercup's hand. She waved the wand in front of Violet.

"I'll give you hiccups that last forever!" Buttercup said.

Violet closed her eyes. She hoped something would happen before she got the hiccups again.

She got her wish.

"Happy Halloween!"

Bogey Bill crashed through the ceiling.

Violet hadn't gotten a good look at the goblin before. But now she did.

His skin was gray and scaly. He was bald. He had long, thin fingers and toes.

Bogey Bill stuck out his tongue and made a terrible face. His eyes popped out of his head. His pointy ears grew big.

"Eeeeeeeeeeek!" screamed Buttercup.

Chapter Ten
Get That Goblin!

"We did it!" Violet said. "Buttercup is scared!"

A whooshing sound filled the air. A tunnel of wind appeared out of nowhere. The wind sucked Buttercup inside.

"I love hiccups!" Buttercup yelled. "Is that so w-w-r-o-n-n-g-g . . . ?"

Then the room was quiet. Buttercup and the tunnel vanished.

"All right!" Leon yelled.

But it wasn't over yet.

Bogey Bill looked at them.

"You tricked Buttercup," the goblin said. Violet thought his voice sounded like a bullfrog's croak. "You sent her back to the Otherworld."

Sprite took a medal out of his bag. "That's right!" Sprite said. "I'm a Royal Pixie Tricker. Just like it says here."

Bogey Bill laughed.

"S-s-sorry we tricked your friend," Leon said, looking at the goblin. "I hope you're not mad at us or anything."

Bogey Bill scowled. "She wasn't my friend. So pretty and cute. Yuck!"

"But wasn't she kind of sweet?" Violet asked.

Bogey Bill stuck out his tongue. "Yuck. Like a flower. Bogey Bill hates flowers."

"You do?" Violet asked. Her heart sank. She'd thought she'd be able to get the goblin to say something sweet about Buttercup. But she was wrong.

"I do hate flowers," Bill said. "But do you know what I hate even more?"

Violet shook her head.

"Fluffy bunnies!" Bogey Bill shouted. He threw some pixie dust in the air.

Then he disappeared.

"What was he talking about?" Sprite asked.

"I don't care," Leon said. "I'm just glad he's gone."

But Violet had a bad feeling.

A very bad feeling.

"Today is the *Fluffy Bunny Baby* special," she said.

"So?" asked Leon.

Sprite flew between them. "So, Bogey Bill will try to ruin it," he said. "He'll make it scary."

"If we don't hurry," Violet said, "Bogey Bill is going to scare every baby in town!"

"And he'll make the whole town crazy with fear," Leon said. "It's just like I said."

Sprite fluttered up and down. "This is very, very bad," he said. "Besides scaring everyone, Bogey Bill might be seen on TV."

Violet paled. "Then everyone would know the secret of the pixies!"

Chapter Eleven
Save Fluffy Bunny!

"Let's go!" Violet said.

Sprite threw pixie dust over them all.

"To the TV studio!" Sprite yelled.

In a flash, Violet, Sprite, and Leon left the haunted house.

They reappeared in a hallway.

"Where are we?" Leon asked.

"We must be in the TV studio," Violet said. "Let's look around."

Leon, Sprite, and Violet tiptoed quietly down the hall.

Violet peeked in one door. A man stood in front of a weather map. He gave the weather report.

"That's the news studio," Violet whispered to Leon.

A man working the lights shivered. "I hope there's not a thunderstorm," said the man. "I'm afraid of thunder and lightning."

They walked to another door. Violet saw a woman sitting in a dressing room.

"I'm not going on the air!" the woman said. "I've got stage fright."

"Bogey Bill must be here," Violet said.

They walked to the next door.

A big pink bunny rabbit stood in front of the cameras. The bunny danced around big fake flowers made of plastic.

"I'm Fluffy Bunny! Come and play with me!" sang the rabbit.

Several men and women stood at the side of the set. Violet guessed they were the crew.

"This is it," Violet said. "Now we've got to find Bogey Bill."

But Leon started to dart out the door. "Count me out!" he said.

"What's the matter?" Violet asked.

"It's that b-b-bunny," Leon said. "It's so fluffy. And pink. And s-s-scary!"

Violet sighed. Bogey Bill's magic was making Leon afraid of Fluffy Bunny!

"We won't let the bunny hurt you, Leon," she said. "Promise."

Violet put Sprite into her pocket. "You'd better stay hidden," she said. "There are a lot of people in there."

Violet and Leon crouched down. They crept into the studio. They hid behind a table.

No one noticed them. They stayed still and watched the show.

Fluffy Bunny finished his song. "Bye, babies! I'll be back in a minute," he said.

Fluffy Bunny walked offstage. Then he took off his big pink bunny head.

Inside the costume was a man with a round, bald head.

"Boy, am I thirsty," the man said in a deep voice. He walked out of the room. The woman behind the camera followed him. The other people in the crew started busily moving around.

"Thank goodness that horrible bunny is gone," Leon said.

"Yes," Sprite said. "Now we can look around."

Violet started to move. Then she stopped.

"We don't have to look hard," she said. "There he is!"

Hiding behind a big fake flower was a little gray goblin.

Bogey Bill!

Bogey Bill was smiling and muttering to

himself. "Happyyy Halloweeeeeen, babies!" croaked the goblin softly.

Chapter Twelve
Sammy Spider

"We've got to do something fast!" Violet said.

"Didn't that gnome guy tell you what to do?" Leon asked. He pulled the stuffed spider from his pocket. "How do we use this thing?"

"He didn't tell us," Violet said. "He said we'd know what to do."

"Maybe it's a magic weapon," Leon said. "Like in a video game."

Sprite flew in front of Leon's face. "Leon, we don't use weapons to trick fairies. We use our heads."

"That's what you say," Leon said. "I'm going to try it my way."

Before Violet could stop him, Leon ran out onto the set. Right behind Bogey Bill.

Violet looked around, worried. Would they be caught? But Leon and the goblin were hidden behind the flower. They were out of sight of the crew.

Leon took the stuffed spider and bopped Bogey Bill on the head.

"Take that! And that!" he said. He bopped Bogey Bill again and again.

"Leon, no!" Violet whispered.

Bogey Bill turned around. He glared at Leon. "What are you doing?" he growled.

And then, suddenly, he smiled.

"Sammy?" Bogey Bill asked. "Sammy Spider, is that you?"

Bogey Bill grabbed the spider out of Leon's hands. He looked into its beady eyes.

Then he hugged it.

"Sammy Spider! My favorite toy!" Bogey Bill cried. "I haven't seen you since I was just a little goblin."

"That must be how Robert B. Gnome got it," Violet told Sprite.

Bogey Bill squeezed the spider tightly. "I love you, Sammy Spider," he croaked. "You're my best friend!"

Violet grinned. "What a sweet thing to say!"

Bogey Bill looked shocked. "No fair!" he said. "I didn't mean it!"

But it was too late. The wind tunnel came for Bogey Bill. It sucked him right up.

"Happy Halloweeeeen!" Bogey Bill cried.

Then he was gone.

"We did it!" Violet said happily. "We tricked him. We saved the show."

Suddenly, Fluffy Bunny's music started up again. Fluffy Bunny ran back into the studio. He put his bunny head back on.

The woman got back behind the camera. Fluffy Bunny hopped out onto the set.

Then Fluffy Bunny stopped hopping.

"Oh, no!" Violet said.

Leon was still behind hiding the fake flower! He stood up.

Bright lights shone in Leon's eyes.

Fluffy Bunny stared at him.

Leon waved at the camera.

"Hi, babies!" Leon said.

Chapter Thirteen
More Trouble?

"Sprite, quick!" Violet said.

Leon ran offstage. Sprite threw pixie dust on them.

"Home!" Sprite yelled.

"Achoo!" said Violet. She forgot to hold her nose.

In a flash, they were safe in Leon's room.

"Did you see that?" Leon asked. "I'm a star."

Leon clicked on the TV. Fluffy Bunny was talking to the camera.

"That was one of Fluffy Bunny's friends," the pink rabbit said. "Fluffy Bunny has lots of friends!"

Violet sank down to the floor.

"That was close," she said. "Sprite, let's look in the book."

Sprite opened up the *Book of Tricks.* He turned to Bogey Bill's pages.

Instead of a blank page, there was now a picture of the goblin.

"Thank goodness," Violet said.

Then Sprite turned to Buttercup's page. Her picture was there, too.

"We really did it!" Violet said.

"You mean *I* did it," Leon said. "It was *my* idea to use that spider."

"That was an accident!" Violet said. Her cousin made her so angry sometimes!

"I'm always saving you guys," Leon said. "You wouldn't have caught Jolt without me. Or Aquamarina."

"That's only because you —"

"Hey, you two," Sprite said. "Stop fighting. We've got a bigger problem." He pointed to the TV screen.

It was a commercial. A man sat in a chair. He looked very tall. He had shiny white hair.

"So vote for me, Wiz Finnster," said the man. "Wiz Finnster for mayor!"

"What's the big deal?" Leon asked. "That's just some old guy running for mayor."

But Violet thought she knew what was wrong.

"Wiz Finnster," she said. "Turn it around. It's Finn the Wizard, isn't it?"

Sprite nodded. "That's him, all right. And if we don't stop him, he's going to take over your whole town!"

"Oh, great," Leon moaned.

But Violet looked down at the book.

They had captured Pix. And Jolt. And Aquamarina.

And today, they had captured two more fairies!

They had Queen Mab to help them. And Robert B. Gnome.

"Don't worry, Sprite," Violet said. "Together, we can do anything!"

Pixie Tricks Stickers

Place the stickers in the *Book of Tricks.* You can find your very own copy of the *Book of Tricks* in the first two books of the Pixie Tricks series, *Sprite's Secret* and *The Greedy Gremlin*. When Sprite and Violet catch a pixie, stick its sticker in the book. Follow the directions in the *Book of Tricks* to complete each pixie's page. (Pixie Secret: Most of these pixies haven't been caught yet. Save their stickers to use later.)